Dear Parents:

Congratulations! Your child is taking
the first steps on an exciting journey.
The destination? Independent reading!

STEP INTO READING® will help your child get there. The program offers
five steps to reading success. Each step includes fun stories and colorful
art or photographs. In addition to original fiction and books with favorite
characters, there are Step into Reading Non-Fiction Readers, Phonics Readers
and Boxed Sets, Sticker Readers, and Comic Readers—a complete literacy
program with something to interest every child.

Learning to Read, Step by Step!

Ready to Read   Preschool–Kindergarten
• big type and easy words • rhyme and rhythm • picture clues
For children who know the alphabet and are eager to
begin reading.

Reading with Help   Preschool–Grade 1
• basic vocabulary • short sentences • simple stories
For children who recognize familiar words and sound out
new words with help.

Reading on Your Own   Grades 1–3
• engaging characters • easy-to-follow plots • popular topics
For children who are ready to read on their own.

Reading Paragraphs   Grades 2–3
• challenging vocabulary • short paragraphs • exciting stories
For newly independent readers who read simple sentences
with confidence.

Ready for Chapters   Grades 2–4
• chapters • longer paragraphs • full-color art
For children who want to take the plunge into chapter books
but still like colorful pictures.

STEP INTO READING® is designed to give every child a successful
reading experience. The grade levels are only guides; children will progress
through the steps at their own speed, developing confidence in their reading.
The F&P Text Level on the back cover serves as another tool to help you
choose the right book for your child.

Remember, a lifetime love of reading starts with a single step!

Visit us on the Web!
StepIntoReading.com
randomhousekids.com
Educators and librarians, for a variety of teaching tools,
visit us at RHTeachersLibrarians.com

Library of Congress Cataloging-in-Publication Data
Lionni, Leo, 1910–1999, author, illustrator.
An extraordinary egg / Leo Lionni.
pages   cm. — (Step-into-reading)
"Originally published in hardcover in the United States by Alfred A. Knopf in 1994."
Summary: Jessica the frog befriends the animal that hatches from an egg she brought home,
thinking it is a chicken.
ISBN 978-0-385-75547-4 (tr. pbk.) — ISBN 978-0-385-75548-1 (lib. bdg.)
[1. Frogs—Fiction. 2. Alligators—Fiction. 3. Friendship—Fiction. 4. Identity—Fiction.] I. Title.
PZ7.L6634Ex 2015
[E]—dc23   2014046728

This book has been officially leveled by using the F&P Text Level Gradient™ Leveling System.
Printed in the United States of America   10 9 8 7 6 5 4 3 2 1

An Extraordinary Egg

by Leo Lionni

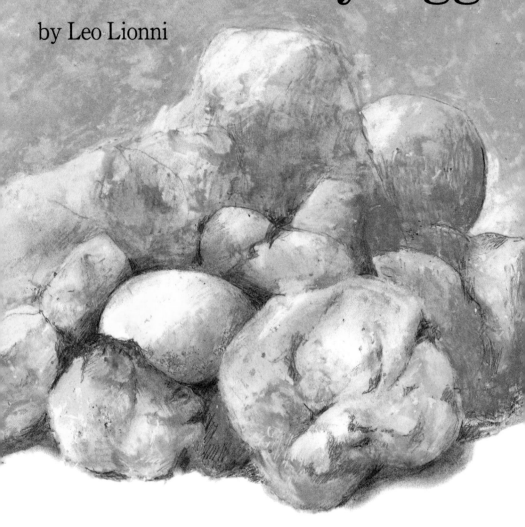

Random House 🏠 New York

4

On Pebble Island,
there lived three frogs:
Marilyn, August, and one who
was always somewhere else.

That one's name was Jessica.
Jessica was full of wonder.
She would go on long walks,
way to the other side of Pebble
Island, and return at the end
of the day, shouting,
"Look what I found!"

And even if it was nothing but
an ordinary little pebble,
she would say,
"Isn't it extraordinary?"
But Marilyn and August
were never impressed.

One day, in a mound of stones,
she found one that stood out
from all the others. It was
perfect, white like the snow
and round like the full moon
on a midsummer night.

Even though it was almost
as big as she was, Jessica
decided to bring it home.

"I wonder what
Marilyn and August will say
when they see this!" she
thought as she rolled the
beautiful stone to the small
inlet where the three
of them lived.

11

"Look what I found!" she
shouted triumphantly.
"A huge pebble!"
This time Marilyn and
August were truly
astonished. "That is not
a pebble," said Marilyn,
who knew everything
about everything.

"It's an egg.

A chicken egg."

"A chicken egg? How do you

know it's a chicken egg?"

asked Jessica, who had never

even heard of chickens.

Marilyn smiled.

"There are some things

you just know."

14

A few days later, the frogs
heard a strange noise coming
from the egg. They watched in
amazement as the egg cracked
and out crawled a long,
scaly creature that walked
on four legs.
"See!" exclaimed
Marilyn. "I was
right! It *is* a chicken!"

"A chicken!" they all shouted.
The chicken took a deep
breath, grunted, gave each of
the astonished frogs a look, and
said in a small, raspy voice,
"Where is the water?"
"Straight ahead!"
the frogs cried
out excitedly.

The chicken threw herself
into the water, and the frogs
dove in after her. To their
surprise, the chicken
was a good swimmer,
and fast too,

and she showed them new
ways to float and paddle.
They had a wonderful time
together and played from
sunup to sundown. And
so it went for many days.

Then, one day, when Jessica
was somewhere else, August
and Marilyn saw a commotion
in the water below them.
Someone was in trouble.
Quickly, the chicken dove into
the dark pool. August and
Marilyn were frightened.

After a few long moments,
the chicken reappeared,
carrying Jessica.

"I'm all right," she called.

"I got tangled in the weeds,

but the chicken saved me."

From that day on, Jessica and her rescuer were inseparable friends. Wherever Jessica went, the chicken went too. They traveled all over the island.

They went to Jessica's secret
thinking place . . .

. . . and to the great
pebble monument.

One day, they went to a place
where Jessica had never been
before. A red and blue bird
flew down from a tree.
"Oh, there you are!"
it exclaimed when it saw the
chicken. "Your mother has
been looking all over for you!
Come! I'll take you to her."

They followed the bird
for a very long time.
They walked and they walked.
They walked under the warm
sun and the cool moon,
and then . . .

. . . they came upon the most
extraordinary creature
they had ever seen.

It was asleep. But when it
heard the little chicken shout
"Mother!" it slowly opened one
eye, smiled an enormous smile,
and, in a voice as gentle as the
whispering grass, said,
"Come here, my sweet little
alligator." And the little chicken

climbed happily onto her
mother's nose. "Now it's time
for me to go," said Jessica. "I'll
miss you very much, little chicken.
Come visit us soon—and bring
your mother too."

Jessica couldn't wait to tell Marilyn and August what had happened. As she neared the inlet, she shouted, "Guess what I found!"

And she told them all about it.

"And do you know what the mother chicken said to her baby?" Jessica asked. "She called her 'my sweet little alligator'!"

"Alligator!" said Marilyn.

"What a silly thing to say!"

And the three frogs couldn't stop laughing.

STEP INTO READING®

with Leo Lionni

A frog leaves the pond to explore the world, but what happens when his good friend, a minnow, tries to follow in his footsteps?